WHAT ARE YOU HUNGRY FOR?

Feed Your Tummy and Your Heart

By Emme and Phillip Aronson ♡ Pictures by Erik Brooks

HarperCollinsPublishers

To John Silbersack of Trident Media Group.
To Antonia Markiet and her fabulous HarperCollins team,
Whitney, Robin, Martha, and Carla: Thank you ever so much for your
wisdom, guidance, and support, and most of all for believing in us.

To Erik: you made us proud.

—EMME AND PHIL

What Are You Hungry For? Feed Your Tummy and Your Heart
Text copyright © 2007 by Emme Associates, Inc.
Illustrations copyright © 2007 by Erik Brooks
Manufactured in China.

Library of Congress Cataloging-in-Publication Data
Aronson, Emme.   What are you hungry for? / by Emme and Phillip Aronson ;
pictures by Erik Brooks. — 1st ed.   p. cm.
Summary: A child describes various foods and non-food treats that make people feel good.
ISBN-10: 0-06-054307-8 (trade bdg.) — ISBN-10: 0-06-054308-6 (lib. bdg.)
ISBN-13: 978-0-06-054307-5 (trade bdg.) — ISBN-13: 978-0-06-054308-2 (lib. bdg.)
[1. Contentment—Fiction. 2. Foods—Fiction.] I. Brooks, Erik, date II. Title.
PZ7.A7429Wh 2005   2003024273   [E]—dc22   CIP   AC

Typography by Carla Weise
1 2 3 4 5 6 7 8 9 10
❖
First Edition

Dear sweet Toby,
May you always grow strong
in your mind, body, and spirit
Love, Mom and Dad

For Keeley Jane, with love

—E.B.

Sometimes I'm hungry for . . .

a **TALL** ice cream cone with sprinkles on top.

But other times, I'd rather have . . .

a *cozy* cuddle
with my dog.

Sometimes I'm hungry for a llllooonnnggg hot dog with mustard and relish and a cold glass of milk.

But other times, a **silly** smile
from my sister hits the spot.

Sometimes I'm hungry for

a CRUNCHY ear of corn

dripping with butter.

But other times, all I want is
a piggyback ride from Grandpa.

Sometimes a pat on the back from my coach
makes everything OK.

But other times, a **GIANT** pepperoni, mushroom, and extra cheese pizza with my team REALLY cheers me up.

Sometimes I want to
snuggle up,
just me and my cat.

But other times, a **BIG** bear hug
from my brother is a great surprise.

Some days it's hard to decide between a
JUICY hamburger with lettuce, pickles,
and lots of ketchup . . .

or maybe a **CRISP** red apple.

But sharing with a friend is good ANY day.

A birthday party with chocolate cake
is always a special treat.

But a belly laugh with my best friend
makes the day even better.

Sometimes, when I'm feeling **blue**,
the only thing that makes me feel good . . .

is a bowl of Grandma's chicken soup.

But the one thing that makes me feel the
best is a hug and a kiss from my mommy
and daddy when they tuck me in at night!

Then I feel JUST RIGHT.